THIS CANDLEWICK BOOK BELONGS TO:

_____

_____

_____

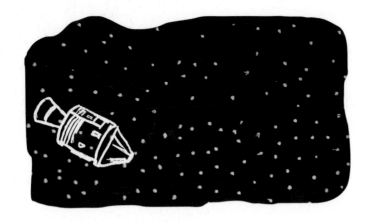

To my mum, Sophie, my greatest hero

First U.S. paperback edition 2021
First published by Otter-Barry Books (United Kingdom) 2019

Library of Congress Catalog Card Number 2019938934
ISBN 978-1-5362-0946-4 (hardcover)
ISBN 978-1-5362-2195-4 (paperback)

21 22 23 24 25 26 TLF 10 9 8 7 6 5 4 3 2 1

Printed in Dongguan, Guangdong, China

This book was typeset in Agenda.
The illustrations were done in acrylic.

Candlewick Press
99 Dover Street
Somerville, Massachusetts 02144

visit us at www.candlewick.com

ASTRO GIRL

Ken Wilson-Max

CANDLEWICK PRESS

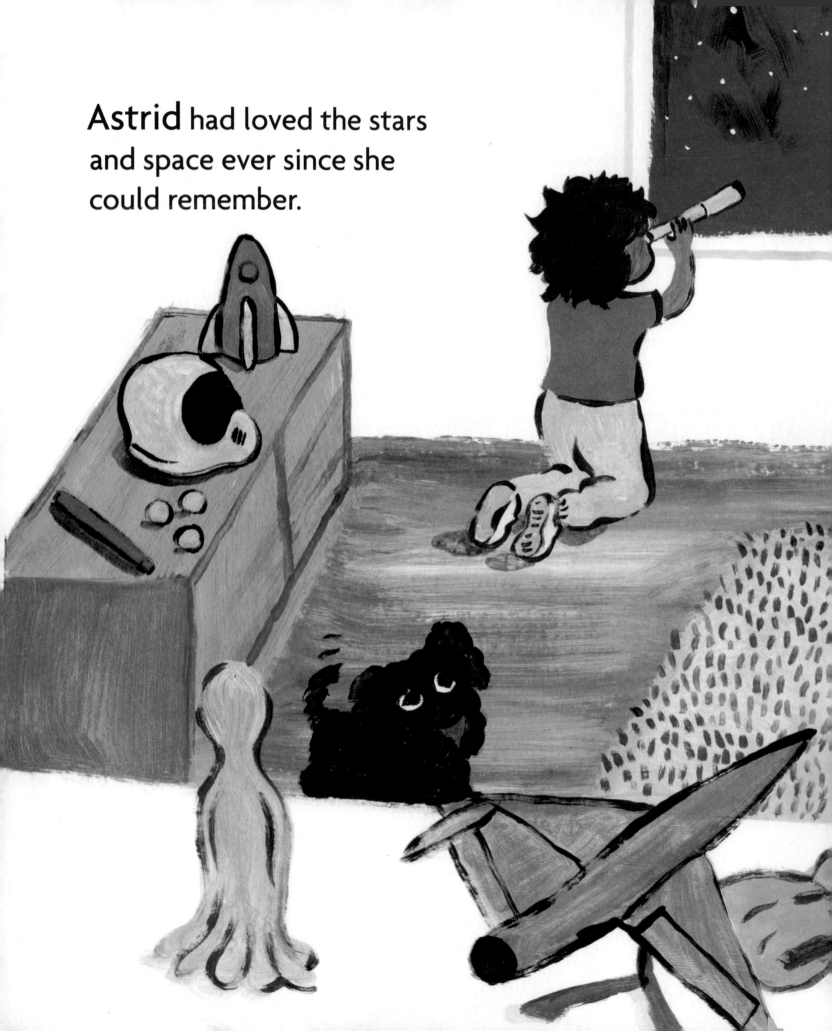

Astrid had loved the stars and space ever since she could remember.

"I want to be an astronaut," Astrid told her best friend, Jake, as they gazed up at the stars.

"Will you bring me an asteroid when you come back from space?" asked Jake.

"Of course I will, Jakey."

"I want to be an astronaut!" Astrid said at breakfast.

"Are you sure?" Papa asked. "You'll have to go round and round the Earth in your spaceship."

He swung her around.

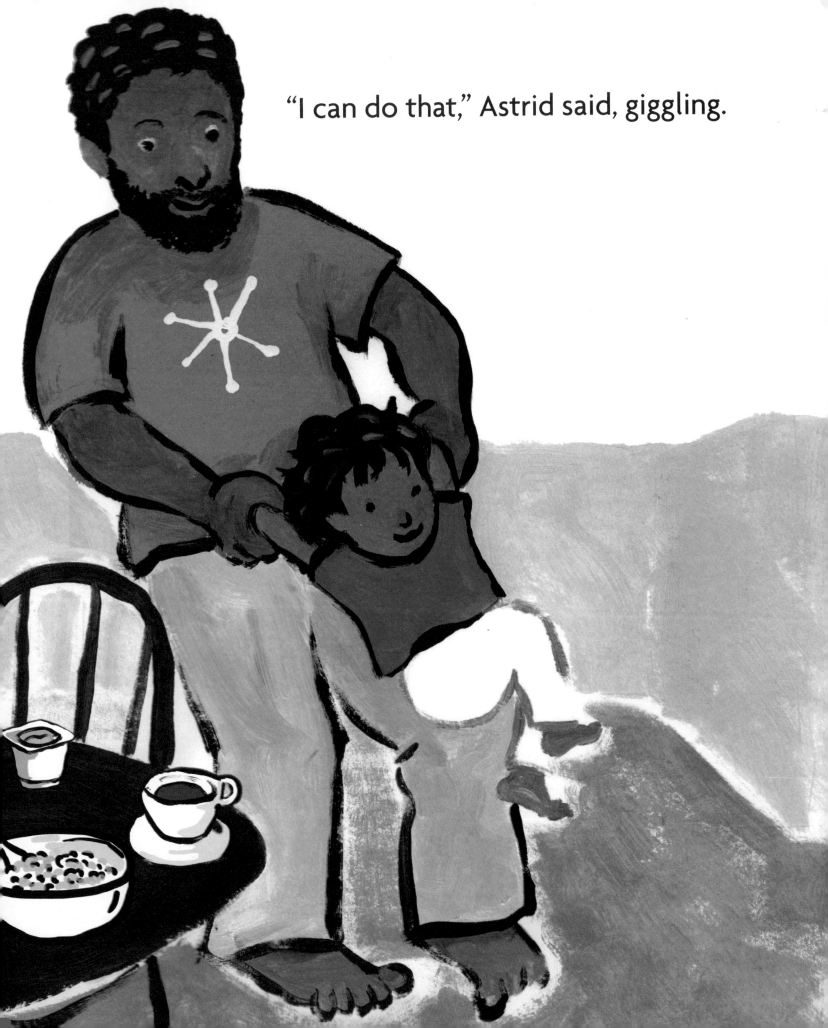

"I can do that," Astrid said, giggling.

"What about eating food out of a tube or a package every day?"

"I can do that," said Astrid as she munched a cereal bar.

"OK, Astro Girl, you'll also have to get used to zero gravity."

Papa threw her up in the air.

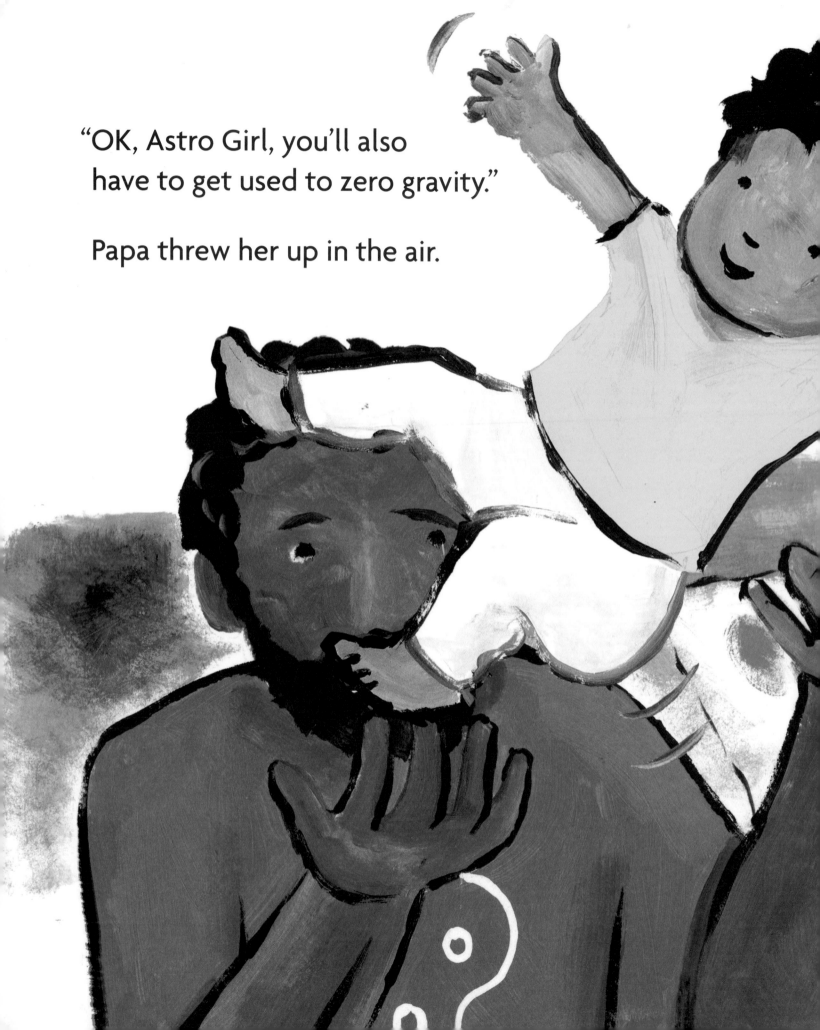

"I can do that all day long!"
Astrid laughed.

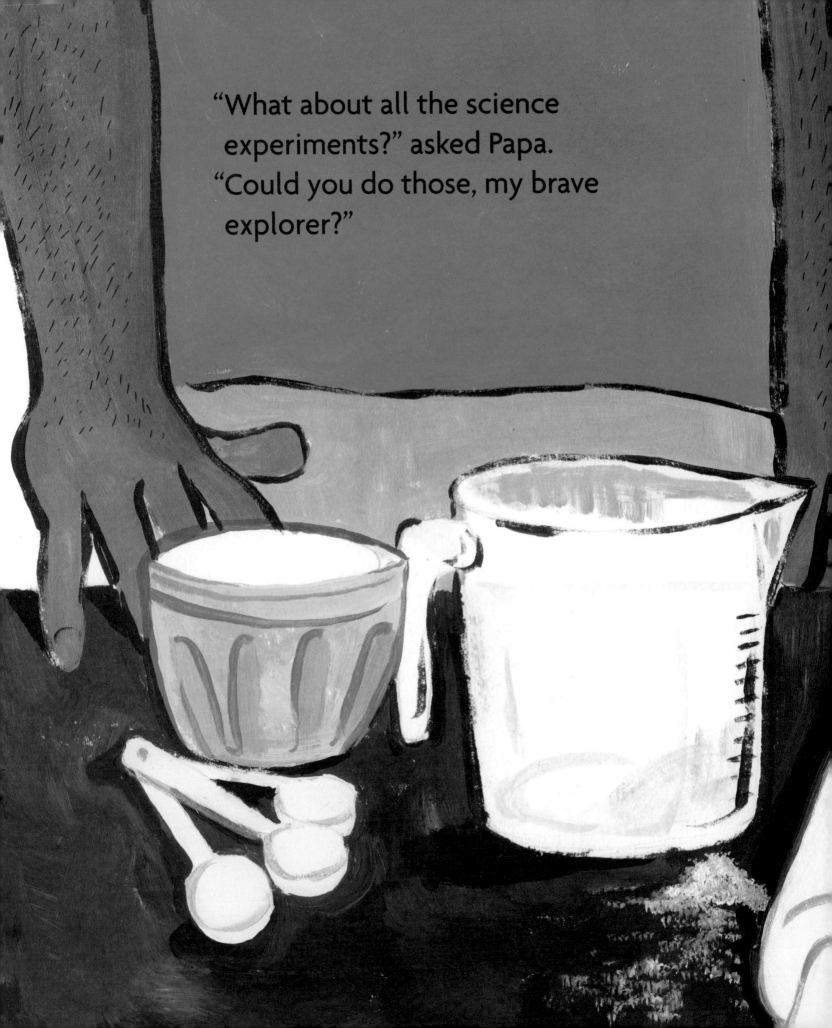

"What about all the science experiments?" asked Papa. "Could you do those, my brave explorer?"

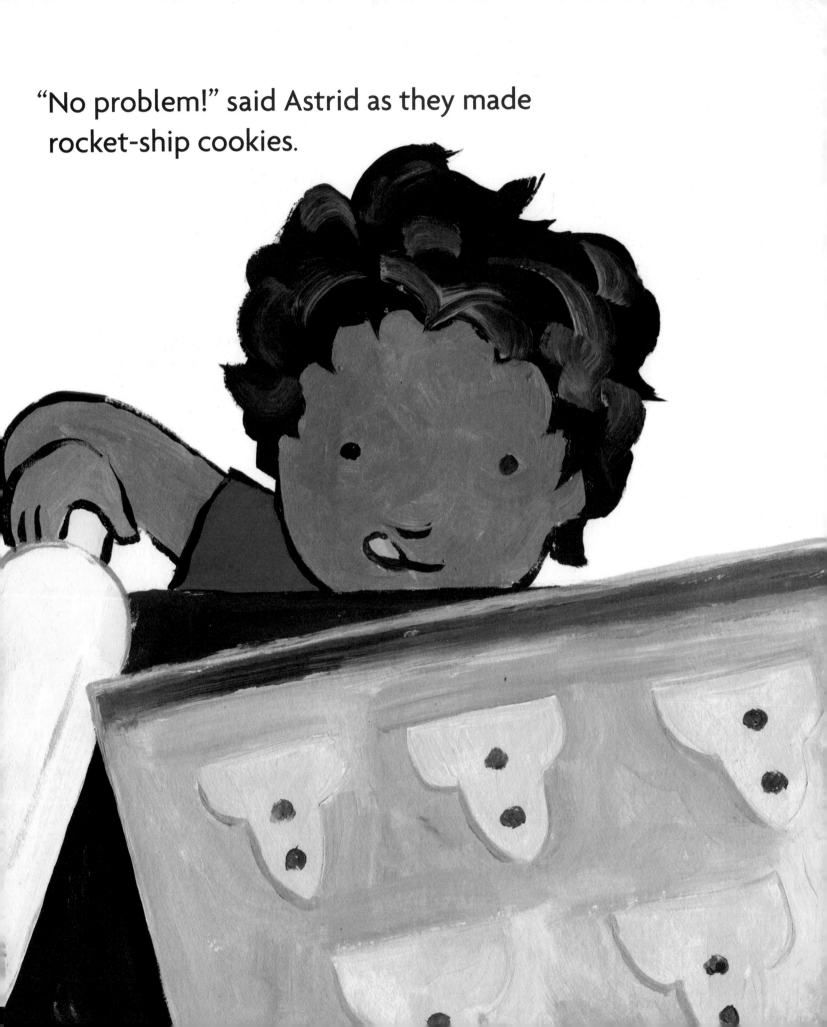

"No problem!" said Astrid as they made rocket-ship cookies.

"Will a space cadet like you be able to sleep on your own among the stars?" Papa asked.

"I think that will be very hard . . . but I'll do it!" Astrid whispered.

At last it was time to go get Mama.
Astrid wore her favorite space T-shirt.

At the space center,
Astrid and her papa
moved to the front of
the crowd just as the
doors opened.

"Mama!" Astrid gave her mama a big kiss.

"I missed you!" said Astrid.

"I want to be an astronaut, just like you," said Astrid. "You're my hero."

Astrid has learned a lot about being an astronaut:

The word *astronaut* comes from two Greek words:
astron, meaning "star," and *nautes,* meaning "sailor."

American astronauts Neil Armstrong and Buzz Aldrin were
the first to land on the moon, in the lunar module *Eagle,*
on July 20, 1969.

The first animal to go into
orbit was a dog named
Laika, on the Russian
Sputnik 2 spacecraft on
November 3, 1957.

Valentina Tereshkova, from Russia, was the first woman in space, in 1963.

Shannon Lucid, from the United States, set a record for the longest time spent in space by a woman (188 days) in 1996.

Mae Carol Jemison was the first African-American woman in space, in 1992.

Helen Sharman was the first British astronaut and the first woman to visit the Mir space station, in 1991.

Kalpana Chawla was the first woman born in India to go to space, in 1997.

Space food is freeze-dried so that it won't spill and cause any damage to machines. Fruit, bread, and nuts are OK as they are.

Astronauts train underwater to create the feeling of floating in space.

Ken Wilson-Max was born and raised in Zimbabwe and studied design in the U.K. He is the author-illustrator of many children's books. He says that he has always believed that people are more similar than different, and that that is worth celebrating. Ken Wilson-Max lives in London.